Where the Wild Geese Go

Where the Wild Geese Go

by MEREDITH ANN PIERCE

illustrated by JAMICHAEL HENTERLY

E. P. DUTTON   NEW YORK

Published in the United States by E. P. Dutton,
2 Park Avenue, New York, N.Y. 10016,
a division of NAL Penguin Inc.

Published simultaneously in Canada by
Fitzhenry & Whiteside Limited, Toronto

Editor: Ann Durell   Designer: Riki Levinson

Printed in Hong Kong by South China Printing Co.
First Edition   W   10 9 8 7 6 5 4 3 2 1

Library of Congress Cataloging-in-Publication Data
Pierce, Meredith Ann.
    Where the wild geese go.

    Summary: In order to save her sick grandmother,
Truzjka embarks on a fanciful journey to find the
answer to the question of where the wild geese go.
    [1. Fantasy]   I. Henterly, Jamichael, ill.
II. Title.
PZ7.P61453Wh   1988   [Fic]   87-24514
ISBN 0-525-44379-7

for J.A.B.,
who said I should do a story
about the vegetable lamb
M.A.P.

for friends,
each a pearl in the sea of memory
J.H.

Truzjka was an impossible child. She lived with her grandmother in a little cottage in the middle of a great, trackless forest. Her grandmother had no patience with Truzjka's dawdles and daydreams. There was always too much work to do and not enough time to do it.

"Truzjka," her grandmother chided while pressing the laundry one day, "you are no help. You eat the berries I send you to fetch, drop eggs, forget instructions, and cannot be trusted to persevere with the churning."

Truzjka, sitting by the open window with the butter churn between her knees, gave the dasher a halfhearted slog.

"I am trying, Grandmother," she murmured.

But what she was really doing was watching a titmouse that had alighted on the windowsill. It was picking up bread crumbs and leaving in the fine dusting of her grandmother's baking flour tiny pairs of stag's-horn tracks.

"Child," her grandmother exclaimed, taking the dasher away from her and churning furiously, "you do enough woolgathering to have an armload of fleece. Do you not realize how soon the hounds of winter will be upon us?"

Truzjka, stumbling out of her grandmother's way, tripped over the milk pail and overturned a basket of eggs on the hearth. Yolks and buttermilk slued in the soot.

"Oh, bother!" the old woman snapped. Forgotten beneath the flatiron, the laundry was beginning to scorch.

Truzjka crept away to fetch a mop-linen.

"My dear," her grandmother scolded that night. "Can you not even manage to comb your own hair?"

"I meant to," mumbled Truzjka. Grandmother's snaggle-toothed comb bit and pulled at the tangles.

"It would be lovely indeed if your head were not a muddle. What's this?" she said suddenly, peering behind Truzjka's ear. "Tsk! Little girls who do not scrub grow feathers."

But Truzjka was not paying any attention. She was off in a daydream, watching the candlelight across the room making her shoe into a sled-shaped shadow. Grandmother kissed her good-night with a sigh of despair.

If it was not one thing, it was surely another. One afternoon a rat got into the house when the old woman was not at home. She returned to find Truzjka hiding behind a stool and the rat having its way with the larder.

"Impossible child!" her grandmother snorted. "When you see a rat, kill it." And she fetched a poker. "Come out," she said, dispatching the rat. "There is nothing to fear."

But Truzjka continued to cower. Truly, an impossible child.

Then one evening in early fall, when Truzjka lay asleep by moonlight, she dreamed the shadows of something passed over her. She dreamed she heard a great hue and a gabble above, as though all the hounds in the world ran yelping through heaven.

She awoke with a start, but peering outside, she saw only gunmetal sky and trees all silvery under the moon. Listening, she heard nothing. The air hung silent as an unstruck bell.

The next morning when Truzjka went down into the kitchen, she found no eggs in the pannikin coddling and steaming, nor nutcakes in the oven turning golden brown. The fire in the hearth was not made up. Her grandmother lay very still in bed.

"Grandmother, what is it?" cried Truzjka, rushing to her.

The old woman moaned. "Last night I saw the wild geese flying and heard them crying their sharp, sad cries. It has pricked my heart till I feel like dying—and if I cannot follow and discover where the wild geese go, surely I will die."

"No, Grandmother!" Truzjka exclaimed as the old woman struggled to rise. "You are too weak. Let *me* find where the

wild geese go. When I return, I will tell you of it, and then you will not die."

"Take care," her grandmother whispered, sinking back. "The way is long. Make plans! Take a warm cloak with you, and a comb, and some journeybread. . . ."

But Truzjka heard not a word she had said. She was already out the door.

Truzjka hurried through the trackless forest. The trees all around her were bright as burning. She gazed through the branches and behind every thicket, but she saw no sign of the wild geese. At last she came to a wide, rolling meadow.

"What beautiful flowers," she told herself. "I will gather a few and take them with me."

Then she plucked for a time, this flower and that, and then a while longer as she ranged farther, gathering other and more beautiful blooms, until an old, gray bellwether grazing nearby lifted his head to inquire: "Are you gathering flowers for your grandmother's grave?"

"No!" cried Truzjka in horror, dropping her nosegay and hurrying on.

Evening came. The woods grew dark. Truzjka shivered and began to run.

All at once she came to a strange little hut made of earth and twigs. A small brown woman stood in front. Brown hair, brown eyes, brown face and hands—she wore a brown garment all covered with berries.

"Please," Truzjka panted, all in a muddle. "My grandmother is very ill. I am trying to find where the wild geese go."

"Tsk!" the little woman said. "And on top of it all, you have run off from home without any plan. Your hair is as wild as a rat's nest, my dear. Come in," she added, holding open the gate. "We must sort it out."

Inside the hut was a vegetable lamb. It grew in an earthen pot by the great hearthstone. Truzjka stared at it. The lambkins at the tips of its branches were no bigger than mice. They were curled up, all of them fast asleep.

"I give them my berries," the little woman chuckled, "and they give me their fleece."

Then she handed Truzjka an old stag's-horn carding comb to straighten her hair and plucked a pippin from her sleeve. It tasted delicious, like perry cider, and soon Truzjka felt wonderfully drowsy and warm.

"Now then," her hostess said, sitting down at her enormous loom and beginning to weave.

The blanket she was making was deeply blue and bordered in white geese with black wingtips, flying. Woven into the fabric, Truzjka saw a cottage in the middle of a wood, an old woman with a poker and a rat in the larder, and a little girl hiding behind a stool.

Truzjka shivered. "I don't like the rat," she whispered to herself. "I am afraid of rats."

"Listen," she heard the berry woman say. "I will tell you how to find these geese."

She tossed the shuttle back and forth, and Truzjka tried very hard to pay attention, but the warmth of fire and the pippin's savor, the light, dreamy sighing of the lambtree beside her and the clack of the loom lulled her so she could scarcely keep awake. The figures on the blanket seemed to wander and shift.

"Can you remember all that?" the other asked her at last.

"Yes," murmured Truzjka, though she really had no idea what her hostess had been saying, so engrossed was she in the endless crossing and crisscrossing of warp and weft.

"Sleep," the berry woman said. "Already I am weaving your way."

And Truzjka slipped at once into dark blue dreams of starlit sky and wild geese winging, the sound of the loom getting into her dreams, and the vegetable lamb snoring softly all night long its tiny, bleating snores.

When Truzjka awoke, it was broad morning. She lay wrapped in the blue lamb's-wool blanket in the midst of a wide, snowy plain. The berry woman and her little hut were gone.

Truzjka sat up with a start. She was utterly lost! She could not remember a word of what the berry woman had told her the night before. Casting about her, she found she still had the stag's-horn comb, and tucked away in one pocket lay a loaf of waybread: dense, dark cake stuffed with berries and nuts. She was desperately hungry.

But before she could even nibble one corner, she heard a distant baying. Turning, she beheld coming toward her a sled all turned up at one end like a shoe and pulled by a large, square dog. The sled halted as it drew alongside her. Its only passenger was a fat white puppy with eyes as black as currants.

"Ap!" the puppy shouted, wagging his tail. "Ap! Ap!"

"Are you lost, girl?" asked the sled dog, who seemed to be the puppy's mother.

Truzjka nodded.

"Ho, ho!" the sled dog cried. "The more the merrier. Take a sip from the little keg under my chin and come along with us."

Truzjka did so, climbing aboard and bundling herself down beneath the berry woman's blanket.

"Call me Gresjinka." The sled dog laughed, hauling on the traces, and off they went, hurtling over the snowdrifts at a frightening speed.

Truzjka did not mind a bit. The sip from Gresjinka's keg made her feel very merry, and the wind tangled her hair wonderfully. Gresjinka never seemed to tire. Her puppy sat on top of the blanket, scratching his ribs.

"What is it?" Truzjka asked him.

"Snow fleas," he muttered, and Truzjka saw a pair of tiny white specks go sailing off. The clear sky above grew suddenly overcast. *"Brr!"* the puppy growled, burrowing beneath the covers. "It's cold."

Ahead, Gresjinka lifted her muzzle. "Ap, have you been scratching?" she flung over one shoulder.

Ap pretended to be asleep. But before long he had crawled on top of the blanket again, scratching furiously. This time Truzjka saw a dozen lacy specks go flying to the winds. The sky grew darker, and the breeze picked up.

"If the wind grows stronger, I cannot keep running," Gresjinka called. "Best heed me, Ap."

But the puppy only yawned and wriggled closer to Truzjka. She put her arms about him to keep him close, but before long he had squirmed free once more and was on top of the blanket, rolling and writhing and scratching himself in a frenzy.

He gave a great shake, and Truzjka saw innumerable white

specks go flying. All at once snow began to fall, and the wind rose to a howl. Gresjinka halted.

"Ap!" she cried. "You have surely been scratching."

The puppy cowered and wagged his tail.

"Impossible child," his mother snapped. "Climb down, girl. The weather has turned."

"But," protested Truzjka, stumbling to the ground, "surely you cannot mean to leave me?" She did not feel so merry now. The sled dog's dram had given her a headache. "How will I find the wild geese?"

"Persevere!" Gresjinka called, and with that, she and Ap and their little sled turned and vanished into the blur of falling snow.

Truzjka stood astonished. The snow was up to her knees, and the wind was bitter cold. She staggered a few steps, blown this way and that, until she fetched up against a tree, and there she huddled with the berry woman's blanket pulled over her head, while the wind sang and wuthered and tried to take the lamb's-wool from her.

But she held on. At long last the gale blew itself out, and the sky grew clear. The dark was the dark of evening now. She

saw that she was in a forest, in a little clearing with snow heaped around her high as a wall.

She was ravenous, and her hair had become a rat's nest again. As she reached to worry one matted snarl, a large rat leaped out and crouched before her on the snow. Truzjka screamed and scrambled back.

"Scream some more," the rat said nastily. "I love screaming."

Truzjka hid behind a tree.

"Now," the rat mumbled to itself, sniffing about, "have we any food? Have we any food? Yes! Yes! Delicious food."

And Truzjka saw with horror that her loaf of waybread had tumbled from her pocket and was lying on the ground.

"No!" she cried, as the rat scrabbled toward it. "If you eat that, I will starve."

"I don't care a bit," the rat replied, preparing to pounce.

Then, before she even knew what she was doing, Truzjka laid hold of the stag's-horn comb and hurled it at the rat with all her force. It struck the creature on its twitching nose, and in a trice Truzjka had darted forward and seized the loaf.

"If you come near me, I shall kick you!" she cried, retreating and cramming her mouth with waybread—for she was very, *very* hungry and did not mean to let the rat have any. "I wish I had a poker," she shouted around the tree trunk. "Then I would *dispatch* you."

"Oh, would you?" growled the rat, rubbing its crumpled nose, its red eyes glowing. Suddenly it loomed as big as a bear,

with great snaggly teeth and a horrid smile. "Pity you have no grandmother to look after you now."

Truzjka grew paralyzed with fright.

"Hold, rat!" a new voice sounded, and Truzjka beheld suddenly in the little clearing a stag pale as silver, with a rack of horns to span her arms.

The rat hissed, fangs bared, and sprang, but the stag drove it back, trampling it to a muss of cobwebs and ashes under his flatiron heels. Truzjka crouched stock-still behind the tree.

"Come out," the stag called gently. "There is nothing to fear."

Hesitantly, Truzjka emerged. "You have saved my life," she said. "How can I repay you?"

The great stag scratched his chin with one heel. "Where is the waybread the berry woman gave you?"

Truzjka looked down at her hands guiltily. There was only one nut left. Nevertheless, she held it up, and the stag bowed his head till his chin whiskers tickled her palm.

"Call me Sylvern," he said, crunching.

Truzjka sighed, casting about at the head-high snow. "What am I to do, Sylvern?" she asked. "I must hurry and find where the wild geese go, but I have lost my way."

"Gallivanting with weather hounds," the stag remarked dryly. He shook his head. "Gresjinka is a fair-weather friend, but Ap always makes it snow. Why did you not do as the berry woman bade you?"

Truzjka blushed, near tears. "I fear I did not attend to what the berry woman bade me—oh, my hair is a rat's nest! I cannot think."

"That is soon remedied," Sylvern replied, and bent his brow once more so that his horns, which were shaped like hands, reached out to her.

Then she felt as though the gentlest of fingers were combing and sorting and unknotting her hair, and braiding it into two fine, smooth braids.

"Now that is done, once for all," he said, "and you need not worry with rats anymore. Climb on my back. I will take you along your way."

Truzjka did so, and they set out through drifts so deep they breasted Sylvern's belly. The moonlight fell very cold and bright, and the northern dancers shimmered above. Sylvern's fur was marvelously soft and warm. She rested her cheek against his back.

"You are very kind to have come to my aid," she murmured.

The stag turned his head. "Do you not know me?" he asked. "Truly, do you not? I am the stag's-horn comb the berry woman gave you." He shouldered through another drift. "You had only to cast it to the ground for me to spring up to your aid."

Truzjka closed her eyes, sorry now that she had not listened more carefully to what the berry woman had said. She resolved to pay closer heed to instructions in future. The night was very still. She and Sylvern traveled till morning. When she awoke, it was to find they had left the woods and come to a great, flat plain of ice. Ghost-white mountains rose in the distance beyond. Sylvern halted, and Truzjka slid to the ground.

"What is it, my hart?" she asked.

He shrugged great silvery shoulders in a sigh. "I am at my end," he said heavily. "It is a pity there was not more waybread left. I could have taken you farther."

He began to grow very small.

"No, Sylvern!" cried Truzjka, throwing her arms about him. "Don't leave me."

He nuzzled her sadly. "I must."

"Stay, Sylvern," wept Truzjka. "I didn't listen. I don't know the way."

He slipped from her grasp. "No matter, my heart," he whispered, his voice now dwindled to the clicking of bone. "You are on the right track."

Then he was a comb again and nothing more. Sadly, Truzjka picked him up and set him in her hair. She felt a bitter pain deep in her breast. She was all alone. Wrapping the lamb's-wool about her, she stared across the icy plain. The moon was just sinking into the far, stark white mountains. She knew that she must cross them to find where the wild geese go.

The featureless plain strayed on and on. Truzjka could not tell how long she had been walking, for the sky had clouded over and hid the sun. She was rime cold and bone weary and did not know how much longer she could go on.

Then all at once she heard a chuffing, a great puffing and a churning like she didn't know what. Something hove into sight ahead of her, and before she could so much as sneeze, it had halted foursquare before her: a great ox, all white and covered with long, silky hair.

"*Huff, chuff,*" he said gruffly. "You are trespassing. Be off!"

Truzjka stared at him. "I am on my way to find the wild geese. . . ." she started.

"No less," whuffed the shaggy ox, pawing the ground, "you are trampling my garden."

Looking down, baffled, Truzjka realized suddenly that the surface of the ice was traced with frost: lacy sprays and delicate fronds, fine plumes and fingers. Her footprints had been scuffing them out.

The white ox stamped. His hoof left no trail. "Only I can pass here without leaving footmarks," he fumed.

Truzjka eyed his broad, dipping horns and his nose as square as a patch of leather, through which he snorted mightily.

"Please forgive me for trampling your field," she said earnestly. "Truly, I did not even see it was here. But if you drive me back, I shall only leave more tracks." She fell silent for a moment and thought very hard. "What you must do is take me across."

"Take you across?" the white ox gusted, shaking his ponderous head and tapping first one horn, then another against the ice. "Take you across?"

"Yes," she answered. "On your back. It is the only way."

He stood still awhile, blinking and blowing great quantities of steam. "Oh, very well," he rumbled at last.

With a sigh of relief, Truzjka folded her blanket and scrambled onto the ox's back. She was utterly weary. They set off at a sullen plod, the ox picking his way among the whorls of white rime and pausing occasionally to graze. Truzjka frowned. The pale, spectral mountains, very far away, seemed to come no closer.

"What is your name?" she asked in a little.

"Snuf! Snuf, the white ox," her sumpter snorted.

"Your hair is very soft, Snuf," she remarked, feeling of the shaggy locks. "Very long and fine." Indeed it was. "I know a berry woman who could weave wonderful things of this hair."

"Is it? Oh, could she?" the white ox puffed back, lifting his head. His step grew lighter. "You are uncommonly civil."

They jogged along at a fine clip then.

When they reached the ice field's edge, it was nearly night. Snuf halted and nodded toward the mountains' foot.

"Follow that trace, and do not leave it," he told her, "and you will find the ones you seek."

"Thank you, Snuf," Truzjka replied, kissing his broad, square nose. She felt well and rested now.

"Mind you do not stray from the track," the white ox said as she turned to follow the slender passage cutting between the tall stone cliffs.

The path was twisty and very steep, and sometimes so faint she could scarcely make it out. The hills shone gravely white, even as a cloud moved over the moon. She thought she heard voices calling her name.

"Come to us, Truzjka," the voices cried. "We are the ones you have sought so long."

Truzjka felt a beat of joy. Surely it was the wild geese! She ran forward along the path and rounded the bend to behold a whole slope covered with snow-white forms.

"Help us," they cried. "We are slipping away. Gather us together again."

Truzjka saw they were indeed sliding away down the slippery slope. She darted forward and grabbed one goose, then another. They did not protest, lying limply in her arms as she carried them back to the safety of the path.

More geese were slipping and crying for help. Truzjka ran after them, snatching them up and filling her arms. She staggered upslope, panting, to dump them on the track. They lay unmoving in a soft, flocky pile. Truzjka shook her head, staring at them.

Then she realized with a start that they were not geese at all, but a great heap of docked lambs' tails, very old and fusty, which the wind had been scattering. Their lambs had long since run away to find their mothers. She heard a thrill of ghostly laughter.

"Horrid things!" exclaimed Truzjka, backing away. "I have been woolgathering. I must keep my mind upon my task if I am to find the wild geese."

She hurried on, resolving to follow Snuf's instructions. The path wound and twisted over the cold, white hills. The moon remained hidden behind its cloud. At last she grew so weary she sank down to rest.

"Truzjka," she heard voices calling. "Truzjka, here we are."

Starting up in surprise and alarm, she saw a gaggle of white geese limping toward her. Their wings were all broken. Their feathers were torn.

"Mend us!" they called to her. "It is your fault we are in this plight."

Truzjka's heart welled up with pity. She had no notion what she had done to harm these geese, but she wanted to succor them. They languished, sighing. She started toward them, but suddenly she remembered what Snuf had told her. One foot on the path, one foot off, Truzjka stopped, frowning. She looked more closely at the smooth, white shapes.

"You are nothing but broken eggs!" she exclaimed. "Nothing can mend you now. And I must find the wild geese."

With a thrum of eerie murmuring, the outward forms of the false geese faded away, leaving only a tumbled basket and ruined eggshells scattered beside the path. Truzjka hastened on.

The cloud continued to hide the moon. As the way slanted downward, the path grew faint. Truzjka halted, uncertain. She could not tell which way to go.

"Truzjka!" came voices ahead of her. "You have passed our tests. You have seen through our impostors and found us at last."

Peering through the darkness, Truzjka made out pale figures ahead. Wild with relief, she sped toward them.

"Catch hold!" they cried. "We are your heart's desire."

All at once, she paused at the edge of the ghostly track. The wind had brought a strange scent to her, like spoilt clabber. She sniffed again.

"You are only unfinished churning!" she cried, drawing back onto the middle of the path. "Someone should have made you sweet butter long ago, but there is no saving you now. Make way! You are not the wild geese."

She heard an angry shriek, like thwarted spirits, and the moon slipped from behind its cloud at last. Truzjka saw a broken butter churn and a dozen white milk pails blocking her path. She picked her way through them. The trace shone before her like a river of silver pennies now. She ran along it, down toward what lay beyond.

When she emerged from the haunted hills at last, the path ended. She had come to a place where the wind was wet and smacked of salt. Below her, a wild, black sea battered itself against a lean, gray shore. The tide was out.

Truzjka picked her way down over huge barnacles. They were large as goose eggs and hard as lime, all silvery rose and veined with blood purple. The moon lit them. Truzjka cast about for the wild geese.

"Where are they?" she wondered, thinking of Grandmother. "Snuf said I should find them. I must!"

She searched until she was too worn to go on, but she could discover no sign of them. The beach was deserted. It held only barnacles. Truzjka began to cry. Her tears fell onto the shells at her feet, and they opened like rose petals.

A tiny goose came struggling out. It was not a gosling. Its beak was silver, its feet were gold, its pinions milk-pale and tipped with black. Truzjka stared at it. Companions followed, emerging from their shells until she stood surrounded by a gaggle of little white geese.

Then, with a sigh like bread-dough rising, they all grew to full size. They settled themselves upon their barnacles and gazed at her with their wine black eyes.

"You are not the tide," one of them said. "Did you splash us with seawater?"

"With tears," whispered Truzjka. "Are you the wild geese I have sought so long?"

The geese all eyed her, and nodded, and bobbed.

"Yes. We are the barnacle geese," they said. "We hatch out of barnacles. Our shadows are ghosts. Our wings are dreams. We nest on the sea of memory."

Truzjka felt weak. She had found them at last.

"Three days I have been seeking you," she said.

"Three days?" they answered. "Three months, more like. Those who follow us lose track of time."

"Three months?" cried Truzjka. "Oh, my poor grand-mother!"

"She is well enough," murmured one of them. "She has forgotten all about us in her worry over you."

"Over me?" Truzjka exclaimed. "I have been gone too long. I must go home at once."

The wild geese all looked at each other and shook their heads. "We fear that is impossible."

"Oh, bother," one of them cackled. "The tide is coming back."

The ghost-pale geese all crowded past Truzjka, hissing and jostling. She spotted something among the barnacles then, half-hidden by sea wrack, something she had not seen before: a little globe, glass-smooth and clear, lit up by the moon—but she could not see inside, for it was full of mist.

"What is this?" she asked, bending down. The globe was cool to the touch.

"It is nothing," the wild geese answered. "It is of no conse-quence. Leave it and stay with us."

Truzjka put it into her pocket.

"What did you mean just now?" she said, straightening. "What makes it impossible for me to go home?"

"You do not know the way."

The wild geese all chuckled and preened their feathers, and Truzjka realized with a start that she had come so far she did not know her way home. What was she to do?

"You could take me," she said suddenly. "You know the way."

The wild geese fluffed themselves and lowered. "We would rather you stayed here," they answered. "You could become one of us and live in a barnacle."

"No," replied Truzjka, very firmly now. "I want to go home to my grandmother."

The geese muttered, consulting among themselves.

"Then you must give us something," they said at last, "for our trouble."

"What would you have?"

"Your hair," they said. "Your beautiful hair that is brown as bear's fur. Give us your hair."

They jostled about her, and Truzjka looked back at them, biting her lip. She did not want to give them her hair, which was fine and smooth now that Sylvern had combed it—but she could see no other way of getting home.

"Every passage has its price," they murmured.

She sighed and told them, "Very well."

Then *snip, snop,* as quick as sheep shears, they had clipped off her long braids close about her ears. Her head felt oddly cool

and light. The geese divided up the strands and stuffed them into their barnacles. The tide came licking up the beach.

"Make haste," they said. "Lay out your blanket and sit in the middle."

Truzjka did so, and each goose dipped to catch a thread. Then with a clamorous yelping and a riot of flapping, bearing Truzjka along with them on the berry woman's blanket, the wild geese rose into the air.

Ghost mountains and frosted fields flashed below them. Truzjka lay back and gazed up at the moon. The sides of the blanket fanned out about her like the midnight sky. Its borders grew indistinct, so that she could not always tell which were the woven geese and which the true geese flying.

Truzjka found herself growing sleepy by moonlight. She saw then that the blue lamb's-wool had new figures on it, many more than she had seen in the berry woman's hut. She saw the sled of the weather hounds, Sylvern tramping the rat, Snuf grazing, the ghostly passage through the hills, and the barnacle shore. She saw a little girl turning into a goose.

Her arm itched. She scratched it, then started up in horror to realize that snow-white pinfeathers were sprouting there.

She plucked them out with a cry. Her arm smarted fiercely. More feathers began to grow.

"What is happening?" she exclaimed in fright.

"You are becoming as we are," the wild geese answered. "All who follow us do."

"But I don't want to be as you are!" Truzjka cried, plucking furiously.

She felt feathers growing behind her ears and tore at them frantically. All around her, the figures on the blanket began to shiver and disappear. The wild geese were tugging out the threads. Snuf vanished, then Sylvern. Gresjinka and Ap followed. Gaps opened between the warp and weft. The blanket was unraveling.

"Help!" screamed Truzjka.

"Peace," the wild geese told her. "Don't pull at your feathers. If your wings are not grown by the time we are done, you will fall."

"Let me go!" Truzjka shouted.

The great trackless forest sprawled below her. The gaps in the dark blue web kept widening. Truzjka snatched and tore at the feathers growing along her collarbone. She saw the roof of her grandmother's cottage beneath her, shining brightly by moonlight.

"There! Set me down—" she started to tell them, but just at that moment the last fraying thread parted. The wild geese beat upward all about her, calling, each bill trailing a tuft of wool, their wings clapping and buffeting like blown laundry.

Truzjka had plucked all her plumage out. Not one quill remained. For an instant, she hung above the house, her arms catching desperately at the cool blue sky. Then she tumbled through air, hurtling head over heels—down through the chimney and straight into bed, where she lay for a long moment, breathless and stunned.

Her pillow had burst with the force of her fall, and the air was full of pinfeathers and down. By the time it had all drifted lazily to the floor, she had fallen deep asleep, the cries of the wild geese still ringing faintly in her head.

Early the next morning, Truzjka smelled delicious things to eat and wandered down into the kitchen to find her grandmother frying mush.

"Goodness, child," the old woman exclaimed, starting up as though she saw a ghost. "You are all over soot."

"I found the wild geese," Truzjka said as her grandmother fetched a warm, wet mop-linen and sponged her face and hands. Her skin felt sore where the feathers had been, but no new ones were growing. Truzjka gave a great sigh of relief.

"You have been very ill," the old woman was saying. "Truly, I feared I might lose you for good."

Truzjka stared at her grandmother, who strangely enough—though weary and worn-seeming—no longer looked on death's doorsill. "Grandmother, what do you mean?" she demanded, puzzled. She felt very hungry and testy and tired. "It is you who have been ill, not I."

The other seemed to pay no attention. She fetched a hearth rug and wrapped it closely about her granddaughter.

"You must take care to stay warm," she said, running her fingers through Truzjka's short, sooty curls. "You had such a fever, I had to crop your hair. . . ."

Truzjka frowned and shook her head. Grandmother was not making any sense.

"I gave my hair to the wild geese," she said. "They wanted me to stay with them, but I made them bring me home."

The old woman began to look very alarmed.

"Oh, but Grandmother," Truzjka cried, throwing her arms about the other then, "I am so glad to be home and to find you well."

Her grandmother spooned a bowl full of golden fritters from the pan. "You must get your strength back," she said distractedly. "Here, child. Eat."

Truzjka ate the hot, crisp stuff all running with milk and butter. She was ravenous. But when she set down her second empty bowl and tried to tell her grandmother where the wild geese go, she found the memory of her journey all unraveling like the berry woman's blanket. She could not catch hold.

"Peace, child," the old woman exclaimed. "No use mooning over such things by daylight. You dreamed these geese."

Truzjka burst into tears. "I didn't! You heard them. I followed. I found them."

"There, now," her grandmother said more gently, patting her cheek. "Anything is possible, child."

Truzjka dried her tears, but she was miserable still. She could hardly remember the wild geese or her trek.

"To bed with you," her grandmother said.

"But Grandmother," answered Truzjka, astonished. "Do you not want me to go fetch the eggs, or churn the butter, or tend the hearth?"

"Time enough," the old woman replied. "You have lately been feverish. Putting you back to work too soon would coddle your brains for sure. Rest."

Truzjka wandered back to her room, but her bed was a mess of soot and feathers. The stag's-horn comb lay on the pillow where her head had rested. She felt a twinge of memory, but could not catch it. She picked up the comb and set it in her hair.

Then she donned her warmest cloak and cap and crept past

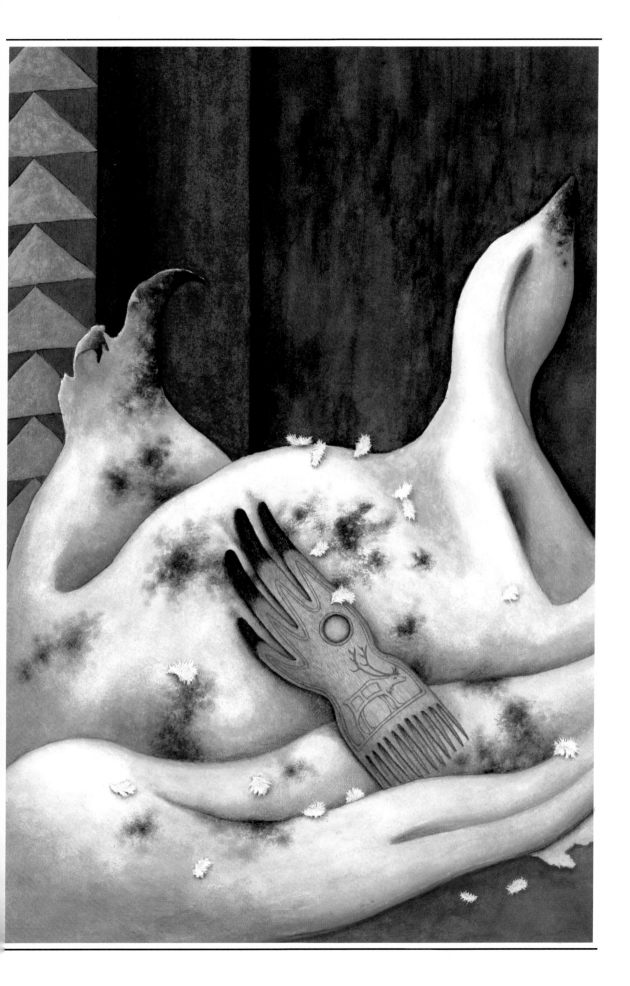

her grandmother, who was sweeping the hearth. Outside, the snow was falling thick as sifted sugar. The sun was a pale disk; it was high winter now, no longer fall. Truzjka didn't feel a bit feverish, only tired, and the cloak and cap kept her toasty-roasty.

"Why can I not remember?" she wondered. "Where has the tell of my journey gone?"

Something in her pocket moved. Reaching inside, she drew out the little globe that she had found among the barnacles. It had been cool then. Now it grew warm in her hands. The mist cleared. She could see inside.

What she saw was the vegetable lamb snoozing beside the fire, and the weather hounds gallivanting, and the white ox grazing and guarding his frost. The smack of salt came into her mouth, and the taste of waybread and perry cider. Holding the globe to her ear, she heard faintly Snuf snorting and Gresjinka baying, the lambkins snoring and the great loom clacking. Memory stirred in her.

"Oh, berry woman," she whispered, "where are you?"

"I am right here, child," the berry woman said.

And looking down into the globe, Truzjka saw once more the little hut of earth and grass. The vegetable lamb was now awake, its branches bent down and the lambkins grazing on the moss that grew upon the great hearthstone. The berry woman perched at her loom.

"What is it I have brought back with me?" Truzjka asked.

The other laughed. "Don't you know? It is a pearl from the sea of memory. Keep it close and treasure it: it is worth a trove."

Truzjka frowned. "And what are you, berry woman?"

"I am the one that weaves your way," the little woman answered. "Like dreams, I am real. And as long as you keep this pearl, you will not lose me, or the remembrance of where the wild geese go."

"They coveted my hair," murmured Truzjka. "Why?"

"Oh, they line their nests with maidens' hair, and bits of lamb's-wool, and the ravels of dreams. Do not worry about your hair, my dear," the nut-brown woman said, gently teasing a tuft of fleece from the back of one of her bleating lambs. "It will grow back straighter now. Sylvern has seen to that."

"Sylvern," breathed Truzjka, remembering suddenly. Her fingers tightened upon the globe. "Berry woman, give me some of your waybread. I want Sylvern back."

"Certainly, my dear," the little woman said, fetching a loaf out of the sleeve of her garment and handing it up through the glass.

Truzjka held it to her nose and smelled its dark, rich scent.

"Call him up whenever you like," the other added. "Only pity your poor grandmother, who just now got you back. Wait till spring before you go traveling again."

Truzjka smiled and stowed the waybread. She nodded.

"Look deep," the berry woman said. "What do you see?"

The image of her hut faded. She faded, and Truzjka bent closer, gazing into the pearl. It felt smooth and weighty in her hands.

Faint and far, she heard a wild clamor, like hounds, which pricked her to the heart. She smelled sea wrack and tasted buttermilk. She saw moonlight, and snow falling, and ghost-white geese with burnt wingtips flying.

They turned black as hearth soot crossing the moon.